Illustration copyright © 1985 Verlag Neugebauer Press, Salzburg.
Published in USA by Picture Book Studio USA,
an imprint of Neugebauer Press USA, Inc.
Distributed by Alphabet Press, Natick, MA.
Distributed in Canada by Vanwell Publishing, St. Catharines, Ont.
Published in U.K. by Neugebauer Press Publishing Ltd., London.
All rights reserved.
Printed in Austria

LIBRARY OF CONGRESS CATALOGING IN PUBLICATION DATA

Nesbit, E. (Edith), 1858-1924.
The deliverers of their country.

Summary: Two youngsters save their country from
a plague of dragons.
[1. Dragons—Fiction] I. Zwerger, Lisbeth, ill.
II. Title.
PZ7.N43777De   1985   [E]   85-9389
ISBN 0-88708-005-7

Ask your bookseller for these other PICTURE BOOK STUDIO books
illustrated by Lisbeth Zwerger:

THE GIFT OF THE MAGI by O. Henry
HANSEL AND GRETEL by The Brothers Grimm
THE LEGEND OF ROSEPETAL by Clemens Brentano
LITTLE RED CAP by The Brothers Grimm
THE NIGHTINGALE by Hans Christian Andersen
THE SELFISH GIANT by Oscar Wilde
THE SEVEN RAVENS by The Brothers Grimm
THE STRANGE CHILD by E.T.A. Hoffmann
THE NUTCRACKER by E.T.A. Hoffmann
THE SWINEHERD by Hans Christian Andersen
THUMBELINE by Hans Christian Andersen

Edith Nesbit THE
DELIVERERS
OF THEIR
COUNTRY
Lisbeth Zwerger

PICTURE BOOK STUDIO USA

It all began with Effie's getting something in her eye. It hurt very much indeed, and it felt something like a red-hot spark – only it seemed to have legs as well, and wings like a fly. Effie rubbed and cried – not real crying, but the kind your eye does all by itself without your being miserable inside your mind – and then she went to her father to have the thing in her eye taken out. Effie's father was a doctor, so of course he knew how to take things out of eyes – he did it very cleverly with a soft paintbrush dipped in castor-oil. When he had got the thing out, he said:

"This is very curious." Effie had often got things in her eye before, and her father had always seemed to think it was natural – rather tiresome and naughty perhaps, but still natural. He had never before thought it curious. She stood holding her handkerchief to her eye, and said:

"I don't believe it's out." People always say this when they have something in their eyes.

"Oh, yes, it's *out*," said the doctor – "here it is on the brush. This is very interesting."

Effie had never heard her father say that about anything that she had any share in. She said, "*What?*"

The doctor carried the brush very carefully across the room, and held the point of it under his microscope – then he twisted the brass screws of the microscope, and looked through the top with one eye.

"Dear me," he said. "Dear, *dear* me! Four well-developed limbs; a long caudal appendage; five toes, unequal in length, almost like one of the Lacertidae, yet there are traces of wings." The creature under his eye wriggled a little in the castor-oil, and he went on: "Yes; a bat-like wing. A new specimen, undoubtedly. Effie, run round to the professor and ask him to be kind enough to step in for a few minutes."

"You might give me a sixpence, daddy," said Effie, "because I did bring you the new specimen. I took great care of it inside my eye; and my eye *does* hurt."

The doctor was so pleased with the new specimen that he gave Effie a shilling, and presently the professor stepped round. He stayed to lunch, and he and the doctor quarrelled very happily all the afternoon about the name and the family of the thing that had come out of Effie's eye.

But at tea-time another thing happened. Effie's brother Harry fished some-thing out of his tea, which he thought at first was an earwig. He was just getting ready to drop it on the floor, and end its life in the usual way, when it shook itself in the spoon – spread two wet wings, and flopped on to the table-cloth. There it sat stroking itself with its feet and stretching its wings, and Harry said: "Why, it's a tiny newt!"

The professor leaned forward before the doctor could say a word. "I'll give you half a crown for it, Harry, my lad," he said, speaking very fast; and then he picked it up carefully on his handkerchief.

"It is a new specimen," he said, "and finer than yours, doctor."

It was a tiny lizard, about half an inch long – with scales and wings.

So now the doctor and the professor each had a specimen, and they were both very pleased. But before long these specimens began to seem less valuable. For the next morning, when the knife-boy was cleaning the doctor's boots, he suddenly dropped the brushes and the boot and the blacking, and screamed out that he was burnt.

And from inside the boot came crawling a lizard as big as a kitten, with large, shiny wings.

"Why," said Effie, "I know what it is. It is a dragon like St. George killed."

And Effie was right. That afternoon Towser was bitten in the garden by a dragon about the size of a rabbit, which he had tried to chase, and next morning, all the papers were full of the wonderful "winged lizards" that were appearing all over the country. The papers would not call them dragons, because of course, no one believes in dragons nowadays – and at any rate the papers were not going to be so silly as to believe in fairy stories.

At first there were only a few, but in a week or two the country was simply running alive with dragons of all sizes, and in the air you could sometimes see them as thick as a swarm of bees. They all looked alike except as to size. They were green with scales, and they had four legs and a long tail and great wings like bats' wings, only the wings were a pale, half-transparent yellow, like the gear-cases on bicycles.

And they breathed fire and smoke, as all proper dragons must, but still the newspapers went on pretending they were lizards, until the editor of

"The Standard" was picked up and carried away by a very large one, and then the other newspaper people had not anyone left to tell them what they ought not to believe. So that when the largest elephant in the Zoo was carried off by a dragon, the papers gave up pretending – and put: "Alarming Plague of Dragons" at the top of the paper.

And you have no idea how alarming it was, and at the same time how aggravating. The large-sized dragons were terrible certainly, but when once you had found out that the dragons always went to bed early because they were afraid of the chill night air, you had only to stay in-doors all day, and you were pretty safe from the big ones. But the smaller sizes were a perfect nuisance. The ones as big as earwigs got in the soap, and they got in the butter. The ones as big as dogs got in the bath, and the fire and smoke inside them made them steam like anything when the cold water tap was turned on, so that careless people were often scalded quite severely. The ones that were as large as pigeons would get into work-baskets or corner drawers, and bite you when you were in a hurry to get a needle or a handkerchief. The ones as big as sheep were easier to avoid, because you could see them coming; but when they flew in at the windows and curled up under your eiderdown, and you did not find them till you went to bed, it was always a shock. The ones this size did not eat people, only lettuces, but they always scorched the sheets and pillowcases dreadfully.

Of course, the County Council and the police did everything that could be done: it was no use offering the hand of the Princess to anyone who killed a dragon. This way was all very well in olden times – when there was only one dragon and one Princess; but now there were far more dragons than Princesses – although the Royal Family was a large one. And besides, it would have been mere waste of Princesses to offer rewards for killing dragons, because everybody killed as many dragons as they could quite out of their own heads and without rewards at all, just to get the nasty things out of the way. The County Council undertook to cremate all dragons delivered at their offices between the hours of ten and two, and whole wagon-loads and cart-loads and truck-loads of dead dragons could be seen any day of the week standing in a long line in the

street where the County Council lived. Boys brought barrow-loads of dead dragons, and children on their way home from morning school would call in to leave the handful or two of little dragons they had brought in their satchels, or carried in their knotted pocket-handkerchiefs. And yet there seemed to be as many dragons as ever. Then the police stuck up great wood and canvas towers covered with patent glue. When the dragons flew against these towers, they stuck fast, as flies and wasps do on the sticky papers in the kitchen; and when the towers were covered all over with dragons, the police-inspector used to set light to the towers, and burnt them and dragons and all.

And yet there seemed to be more dragons than ever. The shops were full of patent dragon poison and anti-dragon soap, and dragon-proof curtains for the windows and, indeed, everything that could be done was done. And yet there seemed to be more dragons than ever.

It was not very easy to know what would poison a dragon, because you see they ate such different things. The largest kind ate elephants as long as there were any, and then went on with horses and cows. Another size ate nothing but lilies of the valley, and a third size ate only Prime Ministers if they were to be had, and, if not, would feed freely on boys in buttons. Another size lived on bricks, and three of them ate two-thirds of the South Lambeth Infirmary in one afternoon.

But the size Effie was most afraid of was about as big as your dining-room, and that size ate *little girls and boys*.

At first Effie and her brother were quite pleased with the change in their lives. It was so amusing to sit up all night instead of going to sleep, and to play in the garden lighted by electric lamps. And it sounded so funny to hear mother say, when they were going to bed:

"Good-night, my darlings, sleep sound all day, and don't get up too soon. You must not get up before it's *quite* dark. You wouldn't like the nasty dragons to catch you."

But after a time they got very tired of it all: they wanted to see the flowers and trees growing in the fields, and to see the pretty sunshine out of doors, and not just through glass windows and patent dragon-proof curtains. And they wanted to play on the grass, which they were

not allowed to do in the electric-lamp-lighted garden because of the night-dew.

And they wanted so much to get out, just for once, in the beautiful, bright, dangerous daylight, that they began to try and think of some reason why they *ought* to go out. Only they did not like to disobey their mother.

But one morning their mother was busy preparing some new dragon poison to lay down in the cellars, and their father was bandaging the hand of the boot-boy which had been scratched by one of the dragons who liked to eat Prime Ministers when they were to be had, so nobody remembered to say to the children:

"Don't get up till it is quite dark!"

"Go now," said Harry; "it would not be disobedient to go. And I know exactly what we ought to do, but I don't know how we ought to do it."

"What ought we to do?" said Effie.

"We ought to wake St. George, of course," said Harry. "He was the only person in his town who knew how to manage dragons; the people in the fairy tales don't count. But St. George is a real person, and he is only asleep, and he is waiting to be waked up. Only nobody believes in St. George now. I heard father say so."

"*We* do," said Effie.

"Of course we do. And don't you see, Ef, that's the very reason why we could wake him? You can't wake people if you don't believe in them, can you?"

Effie said no, but where could they find St. George?

"We must go and look," said Harry, boldly. "You shall wear a dragon-proof frock, made of stuff like the curtains. And I will smear myself all over with the best dragon poison, and – "Effie clasped her hands and skipped with joy, and cried:

"Oh, Harry! I know where we can find St. George! In St. George's church, of course."

"Um," said Harry, wishing he had thought of it for himself, "you have a little sense sometimes, for a girl."

So next afternoon quite early, long before the beams of sunset announced the coming night, when everybody would be up and working, the two

children got out of bed. Effie wrapped herself in a shawl of dragon-proof muslin – there was no time to make the frock – and Harry made a horrid mess of himself with the patent dragon poison. It was warranted harmless to infants and invalids, so he felt quite safe.

Then they took hands and set out to walk to St. George's Church. As you know, there are many St. George's churches, but, fortunately, they took the turning that leads to the right one, and went along in the bright sunlight, feeling very brave and adventurous.

There was no one about in the streets except dragons and the place was simply swarming with them. Fortunately none of the dragons were just the right size for eating little boys and girls, or perhaps this story might have had to end here. There were dragons on the pavement, and dragons on the road-way, dragons basking on the front-door steps of public buildings, and dragons preening their wings on the roof in the hot afternoon sun. The town was quite green with them. Even when the children had got out of the town and were walking in the lanes, they noticed that the fields on each side were greener than usual with the scaly legs and tails; and some of the smaller sizes had made themselves asbestos nests in the flowering hawthorn hedges.

Effie held her brother's hand very tight, and once when a fat dragon flopped against her ear she screamed out, and a whole flight of green dragons rose from the field at the sound, and sprawled away across the sky. The children could hear the rattle of their wings as they flew.

"Oh, I want to go home," said Effie.

"Don't be silly," said Harry. "Surely you haven't forgotten about the Seven Champions and all the princes. People who are going to be their country's deliverers never scream and say they want to go home."

"And are we," asked Effie – "deliverers, I mean?"

"You'll see," said her brother, and on they went.

When they came to St. George's Church they found the door open, and they walked right in – but St. George was not there, so they walked round the churchyard outside, and presently they found the great stone tomb of St. George, with the figure of him carved in marble outside, in his armour and helmet, and with his hands folded on his breast.

"How ever can we wake him?" they said.

Then Harry spoke to St. George – but he would not answer; and he called, but St. George did not seem to hear; and then he actually tried to waken the great dragon-slayer by shaking his marble shoulders. But St. George took no notice.

Then Effie began to cry, and she put her arms round St. George's neck as well as she could for the marble, which was very much in the way at the back, and she kissed the marble face and she said:

"Oh, dear, good, kind St. George, please wake up and help us."

And at that St. George opened his eyes sleepily, and stretched himself and said: "What's the matter, little girl?"

So the children told him all about it; he turned over in his marble and leaned on one elbow to listen. But when he heard that there were so many dragons he shook his head.

"It's no good," he said, "they would be one too many for poor old George. You should have waked me before. I was always for a fair fight – one man one dragon, was my motto."

Just then a flight of dragons passed overhead, and St. George half drew his sword.

But he shook his head again, and pushed the sword back as the flight of dragons grew small in the distance.

"I can't do anything," he said; "things have changed since my time. St. Andrew told me about it. They woke him up over the engineers' strike, and he came to talk to me. He says everything is done by machinery now; there must be some way of settling these dragons. By the way, what sort of weather have you been having lately?"

This seemed so careless and unkind that Harry would not answer, but Effie said, patiently, "It has been very fine. Father says it is the hottest weather there has ever been in this country."

"Ah, I guessed as much," said the Champion, thoughtfully. "Well, the only thing would be... dragons can't stand wet and cold, that's the only thing. If you could find the taps." St. George was beginning to settle down again on his stone slab. "Good-night, very sorry I can't help you," he said, yawning behind his marble hand.

"Oh, but you can," cried Effie. "Tell us – what taps?"

"Oh, like in the bathroom," said St. George, still more sleepily; "and there's a looking-glass, too; shows you all the world and what's going on. St. Denis told me about it; said it was a very pretty thing. I'm sorry I can't – good-night."

And he fell back into his marble and was fast asleep again in a moment.

"We shall never find the taps," said Harry. "I say, wouldn't it be awful if St. George woke up when there was a dragon near, the size that eats champions?"

Effie pulled off her dragon-proof veil. "We didn't meet any the size of the dining-room as we came along," she said; "I daresay we shall be quite safe." So she covered St. George with the veil, and Harry rubbed off as much as he could of the dragon poison on to St. George's armour, so as to make everything quite safe for him.

"We might hide in the church till it is dark," he said, "and then –"

But at that moment a dark shadow fell on them, and they saw that it was a dragon exactly the size of the dining-room at home.

So then they knew that all was lost. The dragon swooped down and caught the two children in his claws; he caught Effie by her green silk sash, and Harry by the little point at the back of his Eton jacket – and then, spreading his great yellow wings, he rose into the air, rattling like a third-class carriage when the brake is hard on.

"Oh, Harry," said Effie, "I wonder when he will eat us!" The dragon was flying across woods and fields with great flaps of his wings that carried him a quarter of a mile at each flap.

Harry and Effie could see the country below, hedges and rivers and churches and farmhouses flowing away from under them, much faster than you see them running away from the sides of the fastest express train.

And still the dragon flew on. The children saw other dragons in the air as they went, but the dragon who was as big as the dining-room never stopped to speak to any of them, but just flew on quite steadily.

"He knows where he wants to go," said Harry. "Oh, if he would only drop us before he gets there!"

But the dragon held on tight, and he flew and flew until at last, when the children where quite giddy, he settled down, with a rattling of all his scales, on the top of a mountain. And he lay there on his great green scaly side, panting, and very much out of breath, because he had come such a long way. But his claws were fast in Effie's sash and the little point at the back of Harry's Eton jacket.

Then Effie took out the knife Harry had given her on her birthday. It only cost sixpence to begin with, and she had had it a month, and it never could sharpen anything but slate-pencils; but somehow she managed to make that knife cut her sash in front, and crept out of it, leaving the dragon with only a green silk bow in one of his claws. That knife would never have cut Harry's jacket-tail off, though, and when Effie had tried for some time she saw that this was so, and gave it up. But with her help Harry managed to wriggle quietly out of his sleeves, so that the dragon had only an Eton jacket in his other claw. Then the children crept on tiptoe to a crack in the rocks and got in. It was much too narrow for the dragon to get in also, so they stayed in there and waited to make faces at the dragon when he felt rested enough to sit up and begin to think about eating them. He was very angry, indeed, when they made faces at him, and blew out fire and smoke at them, but they ran farther into the cave so that he could not reach them, and when he was tired of blowing he went away.

But they were afraid to come out of the cave, so they went farther in, and presently the cave opened out and grew bigger, and the floor was soft sand, and when they had come to the very end of the cave there was a door, and on it was written: *"Universal Tap-room. Private. No one allowed inside."* So they opened the door at once just to peep in, and then they remembered what St. George had said.

"We can't be worse off than we are," said Harry, "with a dragon waiting for us outside. Let's go in."

So they went boldly into the tap-room, and shut the door behind them. And now they were in a sort of room cut out of the solid rock, and all along one side of the room were taps, and all the taps were labelled with china labels like you see to baths. And as they could both read words of

two syllables or even three sometimes, they understood at once that they had got to the place where the weather is turned on from. There were six big taps labelled *'Sunshine'*, *'Wind'*, *'Rain'*, *'Snow'*, *'Hail'*, *'Ice'*, and a lot of little ones, labelled *'Fair to moderate'*, *'Showery'*, *'South breeze'*, *'Nice growing weather for the crops'*, *'Skating'*, *'Good open weather'*, *'South wind'*, *'East wind'*, and so on. And the big tap labelled *'Sunshine'* was turned full on. They could not see any sunshine – the cave was lighted by a skylight of blue glass – so they supposed the sunlight was pouring out by some other way, as it does with the tap that washes out the underneath parts of patent sinks in kitchens.

Then they saw that one side of the room was just a big looking–glass, and when you looked in it you could see everything that was going on in the world – and all at once, too, which is not like most looking-glasses. They saw the carts delivering the dead dragons at the County Council offices, and they saw St. George asleep under the dragon-proof veil. And they saw their mother at home crying because her children had gone out in the dreadful, dangerous daylight, and she was afraid a dragon had eaten them. And they saw the whole of England, like a great puzzle-map – green in the field parts and brown in the towns, and black in the places where they make coal, and crockery, and cutlery, and chemicals. And all over it, on the black parts, and on the brown, and on the green, there was a network of green dragons. And they could see that it was still broad daylight, and no dragons had gone to bed yet.

So Effie said, "Dragons do not like cold." And she tried to turn off the sunshine, but the tap was out of order , and that was why there had been so much hot weather, and why the dragons had been able to be hatched. So they left the sunshine-tap alone, and they turned on the snow and left the tap full on while they went to look in the glass. There they saw the dragons running all sorts of ways like ants if you are cruel enough to pour water into an ant-heap, which, of course, you never are. And the snow fell more and more.

Then Effie turned the rain-tap quite full on, and presently the dragons be-gan to wriggle less, and by-and-by some of them lay quite still, so the chil-dren knew the water had put out the fires inside them, and they were dead.

So then they turned on the hail – only half on, for fear of breaking people's windows – and after a while there were no more dragons to be seen moving.

Then the children knew that they were indeed the deliverers of their country.

"They will put up a monument to us," said Harry; "as high as Nelson's! All the dragons are dead."

"I hope the one that was waiting outside for us is dead!" said Effie; "and about the monument, Harry, I'm not so sure. What can they do with such a lot of dead dragons? It would take years and years to bury them, and they could never be burnt now they are so soaking wet. I wish the rain would wash them off into the sea."

But this did not happen, and the children began to feel that they had not been so frightfully clever after all.

"I wonder what this old thing's for," said Harry. He had found a rusty old tap, which seemed as though it had not been used for ages. Its china label was quite coated over with dirt and cobwebs. When Effie had cleaned it with a bit of her skirt – for curiously enough both the children had come out without pocket-handkerchiefs – she found that the label said *Waste*.

"Let's turn it on," she said; "it might carry off the dragons."

The tap was very stiff from not having been used for such a long time, but together they managed to turn it on, and then ran to the mirror to see what happened.

Already a great, round, black hole had opened in the very middle of the map of England, and the sides of the map were tilting themselves up, so that the rain ran down towards the hole.

"Oh, hurrah, hurrah, hurrah!" cried Effie, and she hurried back to the taps and turned on everything that seemed wet. *'Showery'*, *'Good open weather'*, *'Nice growing weather for the crops'*, and even *'South'* and *'South-West'*, because she had heard her father say that those winds brought rain. And now the floods of rain were pouring down on the country, and great sheets of water flowed towards the centre of the map, and cataracts of water poured into the great round hole in the middle of the map, and the dragons were being washed away and disappearing down the waste-pipe in great green

masses and scattered green shoals – single dragons and dragons by the dozen; of all sizes, from the ones that carry off elephants down to the ones that get in your tea.

And presently there was not a dragon left. So then they turned off the tap named 'Waste', and they half-turned off the one labelled 'Sunshine' – it was broken, so that they could not turn it off altogether – and they turned on 'Fair to moderate' and 'Showery' and both taps stuck, so that they could not be turned off, which accounts for our climate.

How did they get home again? By the Snowdon railway – of course.

And was the nation grateful? Well – the nation was very wet. And by the time the nation had got dry again it was interested in the new invention for toasting muffins by electricity, and all the dragons were almost forgotten. Dragons do not seem so important when they are dead and gone, and, you know, there never was a reward offered.

And what did father and mother say when Effie and Harry got home?

My dear, that is the sort of silly question you children always will ask. However, just for this once I don't mind telling you.

Mother said: "Oh, my darlings, my darlings, you're safe – you're safe! You naughty children – how could you be so disobedient? Go to bed at once!"

And their father the doctor said:

"I wish I had known what you were going to do! I should have liked to preserve a specimen. I threw away the one I got out of Effie's eye.

I intended to get a more perfect specimen. I did not anticipate this immediate extinction of the species."

The professor said nothing, but he rubbed his hands. He had kept his specimen – the one the size of an earwig that he gave Harry half a crown for – and he has it to this day.

You must get him to show it to you!